Will You Be My Friend?

By
ROY *and* **DORIS NICHOLS**

Illustrated by
PAUL MANGOLD

Sweet Publishing

3934 Sandshell, Ft. Worth, TX 76137

God turned the fields green and put leafy coats on the trees. All the world smiled in the spring sun, but not Skeeter Scarecrow. He looked at the fields and the leaves on the trees. Then he looked at his own clothes. Once they had been bright and clean. Now they were dirty and tattered. Even the tall purple hat didn't feel right on his head. Skeeter was sad and lonely.

"Day after day I stand here and wave at the birds, but that only scares them away. I wish I knew how to make friends with them instead. Birds can fly everywhere. They could tell me about all the things in God's world. I just stand here, stuck in the dirt. I wish I could fly, too. I wish something wonderful would happen to change me into a bird. Then I would have friends."

In the distance he heard a loud rumbling. Skeeter stopped talking to himself and listened.

Dark clouds filled the sky as a spring wind and thunderstorm swept over the hill.

"What's going on?" shouted Skeeter as the wind grabbed him and tossed him into the air.

Suddenly he was soaring up, up, up above the fields and trees, above the road and houses. "I'm flying! I'm flying!" Skeeter shouted. "This is something wonderful."

Far below he saw fields and trees and houses and a church with a tall steeple. "What a beautiful world God has made," Skeeter thought as the wind blew him along. "Look at me!" he shouted to a passing blackbird. "Something wonderful has happened. I can fly like you."

"You'd better be careful," said the blackbird. "I hope you know how to land."

Suddenly, the storm was gone, as the wind pushed the clouds over a distant hill. Skeeter began to fall. Down, down, down he tumbled. Things on the ground grew larger and larger.

"I'm falling!" shouted Skeeter. "This is not something wonderful."

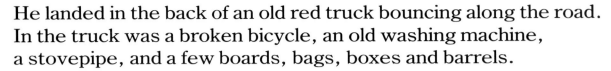

He landed in the back of an old red truck bouncing along the road.
In the truck was a broken bicycle, an old washing machine,
a stovepipe, and a few boards, bags, boxes and barrels.

"Oh, this is awful. This truck is full of junk, and the
farmer is probably taking it to the dump. What will
become of me?" Skeeter grew more and more upset
as the truck rumbled down the road.

At last the farmer stopped and began unloading. One by one he set each thing carefully onto the ground.

"Where did you come from?" he asked as he picked up Skeeter. "I can't sell you at the flea market. You're just a piece of junk. No one will buy a worn out scarecrow." With that he tossed poor Skeeter under a table.

"The farmer's right," thought Skeeter. "I *am* just a piece of junk. I'm not good for anything but scaring the birds away." Skeeter had never felt so sad.

While Skeeter was feeling sorry for himself, people began to gather at the market. Bright umbrellas shaded tables that were filled with everything from books to picture frames.

Suddenly Skeeter heard a happy sound. Was it birds singing? No. It was the sound of children laughing and talking.

"Hello, children," said the farmer. "What are you going to buy today?"

"We don't have any money," said the smallest boy, "but we like the flea market anyway. There are wonderful things to see. Hey, look! What's that under the table?"

"This?" said the farmer, grabbing Skeeter by the neck. "This is an old scarecrow."

"How much does he cost?" asked the boy.

"Oh, he's just a piece of junk. You can have him if you'll just take him away."

"What will they do with me?" Skeeter thought to himself. "Why would they want an old scarecrow like me? Oh, I wish I were back on the hill. At least I could see the birds there, even if they are afraid to talk to me. I'll probably just be torn apart and thrown away."

The children thanked the farmer and put Skeeter into a green cart with two big wheels.

"I wonder where they're taking me," he thought as they bumped along. "I do hope they don't leave me alone in some field or dump me on a pile of trash."

As he listened to the excited children, Skeeter forgot to worry. "They're so happy! I wish I had some friends to talk to. If I could just be friends with the birds, I'm sure I'd be happy. Having friends would be wonderful."

The cart stopped beside a big, brown barrel. "Oh no! They're going to throw me into the trash," Skeeter thought.

But he was wrong. The next thing he knew, he was swimming in warm, soapy water. How good it felt. It was much better than being washed by a cold rain. The children began to scrub, and Skeeter began to smile. The spots on his shirt grew brighter. The yellow of his face shone like the sun, and the old purple hat looked as elegant as a king's crown. Something wonderful was happening to Skeeter.

The children dried him and slipped a beautiful green coat over his long arms. On his feet they placed large brown shoes so he could stand straight and tall. In the purple hat, one of the boys put a bright flower to match the spots on Skeeter's shirt.

After the smallest child had rolled the pants into cuffs, she hugged Skeeter and said, "I love you. You're a friendly, happy scarecrow."

A warm, tingling feeling began in the soles of the old brown shoes and slowly filled Skeeter, right to the top of his hat. As he stood wondering what was happening to him, the children stuffed something into his pockets, the brim of his hat and the cuffs of his pants. They even filled the tops of his old brown shoes. What was going on?

Suddenly, all kinds of birds were flying toward him. They all began to chatter. Robins, sparrows, blackbirds and wrens began to sing, "Skeeter, you're our friend." The children had stuffed food for the birds into his clothes! He was no longer a scarecrow; he was a birdfeeder! He wasn't a piece of junk; he had an important job to do! And he had more friends than he could count!

Now Skeeter understood. He could make friends by helping others. As the bluebird whispered in his ear, Skeeter's smile grew brighter and brighter. "Oh, yes," said Skeeter, "I would love to be your friend."